BEAUTIFUL CREATURES

BEAUTIFUL CREATURES

DAD ISN'T COMING OUT TO EAT AGAIN... HE WRITES ALL NIGHT AND SLEEPS ALL DAY. IT'S BEEN THAT WAY SINCE MY MOM DIED LAST APRIL.

OH, LINK'S HERE.

WHAT DO YOU THINK OF MY BAND'S NEW TRACK?

I THINK IT NEEDS WORK.

LIKE ALL YOUR SONGS.

YEAH? WELL, YOUR FACE NEEDS WORK.

LINK AND I HAVE BEEN BEST FRIENDS EVER SINCE HE GAVE ME HALF OF HIS TWINKIE ON THE BUS TO KINDERGARTEN.

I ONLY FOUND OUT LATER IT HAD FALLEN ON THE FLOOR...

LINK'S BAND IS A TRAGEDY. BUT AT LEAST HE KNOWS WHAT HE WANTS TO DO.

ALL I HAVE IS A SHOEBOX FULL OF COLLEGE BROCHURES. I DON'T CARE WHERE I GO, SO LONG AS IT'S A THOUSAND MILES FROM GATLIN. MY DAD SAYS THERE ARE ONLY TWO KINDS OF PEOPLE IN THIS TOWN—THE ONES WHO ARE BOUND TO STAY OR TOO DUMB TO GO. EVERYONE ELSE FINDS A WAY OUT.

I READ ALL THE TIME. BUT I KEEP THAT TO MYSELF. AROUND HERE BOOKS AND BASKETBALL DON'T MIX. WHAT WOULD THE TEAM, MY FRIENDS, SAY IF THEY KNEW?

The War of Northern Aggression

DON'T YOU MEAN THE CIVIL WAR?

GATLIN, SOUTH CAROLINA, ISN'T LIKE THE SMALL TOWNS YOU SEE IN THE MOVIES. UNLESS IT'S A MOVIE FROM FIFTY YEARS AGO.

AND THEN, THERE SHE WAS AGAIN. IN MY ENGLISH CLASS.

SHE READS. IT'S **ONE** OF HER FAVORITES? SHE JUST SAID IT, LIKE IT'S NORMAL.

CAN IT REALLY BE HER?

THE NEXT DAY, I COULDN'T LOOK AWAY.

RUMMMBLE

PATTER

PTTR

Atticus!

HARPER LEE SEEMS TO BE SAYING THAT YOU CAN'T REALLY KNOW SOMEONE UNTIL YOU TAKE A WALK IN HIS SHOES. WHAT DO YOU MAKE OF THAT? ANYONE?

I THINK IT MEANS YOU NEED TO GIVE PEOPLE A CHANCE. BEFORE YOU AUTOMATICALLY SKIP TO THE HATING PART. RIGHT?

IS LENA THE GIRL IN MY DREAMS?

CHAPTER 2

DO AS I SAY. TAKE THAT BACK WHERE YOU FOUND IT AND BURY IT. THEN YOU COME RIGHT HOME.

I DON'T WANT YOU MESSIN' WITH THAT DUCHANNES GIRL ANYMORE, YOU HEAR ME?

I SPENT TWO HOURS WANDERING AROUND SO AMMA WOULD BELIEVE I'D GONE BACK TO BURY THE LOCKET.

WE GOT TRUBS.

WHAT'D YOU HEAR?

JACKSON HIGH'S GOT ITSELF A REGULAR LYNCH MOB THIS MORNIN'. BEEN GOIN' ON SINCE FRIDAY NIGHT. I HEARD MY MOM TALKIN'.

MY MOM, EMILY'S MOM, SAVANNAH'S...THEY'VE BEEN BURNIN' UP THE PHONE LINES. OVERHEARD MY MOM TALKIN' ABOUT THE WINDOW BREAKIN' IN ENGLISH AND HOW SHE HEARD OLD MAN RAVENWOOD'S NIECE HAD BLOOD ON HER HANDS.

. . .

THMP
KNOCK

. . . . . .

NUHH

-UH

THUMP

WHAT ARE YOU DOING?

WAITING.

IT'S GONNA BE A LONG WAIT.

I'VE GOT TIME.

DID ANYONE EVER TELL YOU YOU'RE CRAZY?

NOT AS CRAZY AS YOU, I HEAR.

IN MY POCKET. WHEN AMMA SAW IT, HER EYES ALMOST FELL OUT OF HER HEAD, LIKE IT WAS TRIPLE HEXED.

BUT I FOUND OUT SOME THINGS FROM MY GREAT-GREAT AUNTS THIS WEEKEND. THE INITIALS ON THE LOCKET, ECW, STAND FOR ETHAN CARTER WATE. HE WAS MY GREAT-GREAT-GREAT-GREAT UNCLE.

THEY SAY I WAS NAMED AFTER HIM.

AND THE INITIALS GKD? IT'S GENEVIEVE, RIGHT?

THEY DIDN'T KNOW, BUT IT HAS TO BE. AND THE "D" MUST BE FOR DUCHANNES.

YOU SHOULD ASK YOUR UNCLE.

NO. MY UNCLE WON'T KNOW ANYTHING.

VRMmm-

WOOF

RAVENWOOD'S DOG!!

GRRR

......!!

WILD DOGS CARRY RABIES. SOMEONE SHOULD NOTIFY THE COUNTY.

MRS. LINCOLN?!

PRINCIPAL HARPER WAS JUST TELLIN' ME HE'S PLANNIN' ON OFFERIN' THAT RAVEN-WOOD GIRL A TRANSFER. SHE CAN TAKE HER PICK OF ANY SCHOOL. AS LONG AS IT'S NOT JACKSON.

GRRR..

IT'S OUR RESPONSIBILITY, ETHAN. WE HAVE TO KEEP THE YOUNG PEOPLE IN THIS TOWN SAFE. AND AWAY FROM THE WRONG SORTA PEOPLE.

WHICH MEANS ANYONE WHO ISN'T LIKE YOU?

I'M SURE YOU UNDERSTAND MY MEANIN'. AFTER ALL, YOU'RE ONE OF US. YOUR DADDY WAS BORN HERE AND YOUR MAMMA WAS BURIED HERE. YOU BELONG HERE. NOT *EVERYONE* DOES.

GRRROWL

ONCE I GOT TO CLASS, THE DAY BECAME ABNORMALLY NORMAL.

THAT IS...UNTIL LINK DROPPED ME OFF AFTER BASKETBALL PRACTICE AND I DECIDED TO DO SOMETHING COMPLETELY INSANE.

I LIED TO AMMA. I TOLD HER I WAS GOING TO THE LIBRARY TO VISIT MARIAN, A FAMILY FRIEND, AND TO WORK ON A PROJECT, BUT...

...NOW I'M BACK AT RAVENWOOD MANOR.

THIS IS INSANE.

I SHOULDN'T DO THIS.

WHAT AM I DOING?!

!!

BARK WOOF GRRROWL BARK

BUT I HAVE A FEELING LENA'S UNCLE MIGHT KNOW SOMETHING THAT COULD HELP US...

ETHAN.

......?

ETHAN, COME ON.

COME DOWN, OR I'M COMING UP.

IF AMMA SAW LENA IN HER PAJAMAS IN OUR FRONT YARD IN THE MIDDLE OF THE NIGHT, SHE'D HAVE A HEART ATTACK...AND THEN A STROKE.

......

TMP

I WAS TOO SCARED TO TELL YOU... BUT NOW I'M TOO SCARED NOT TO TELL YOU...

WHATEVER IT IS, YOU CAN TELL ME. I KNOW WHAT IT'S LIKE TO HAVE A CRAZY FAMILY.

......

......

THE PEOPLE IN MY FAMILY, AND ME. WE HAVE... **POWERS.** WE CAN DO THINGS THAT REGULAR PEOPLE CAN'T DO. WE'RE BORN THAT WAY, WE CAN'T HELP IT. WE ARE WHAT WE ARE.

≈sigh≈

YOU HAVE NO IDEA.

IS SHE TALKING ABOUT...?

MAGIC

I'M AFRAID TO ASK.

AND WHAT, EXACTLY, ARE YOU?

CASTERS, LIKE, SPELLCASTERS.

LIKE, WITCHES?

ETHAN, DON'T BE RIDICULOUS.

Phew!

THAT'S JUST A DUMB STEREOTYPE.

LIKE JOCKS.

WHA-?

WE'RE CASTERS. WE ALL HAVE POWERS. WE'RE GIFTED, JUST LIKE SOME FAMILIES ARE SMART OR ATHLETIC.

WHAT WAS I EXPECTING FROM SOMEONE WHO CAN TALK TO ME WITHOUT EVEN BEING IN THE SAME ROOM?

....

...LOOK. SEE THAT WINDOW OVER THERE? THAT'S MY DAD'S STUDY. HE WORKS ALL NIGHT AND SLEEPS ALL DAY. SINCE MY MOM DIED, HE HASN'T LEFT THE HOUSE...

...IT'S CRAZY.

I KNEW I SHOULDN'T HAVE SAID ANYTHING. NOW YOU PROBABLY THINK I'M A FREAK.

THEN THERE'S AMMA, WHO HIDES MAGIC CHARMS IN MY ROOM—*WITH MY SOCKS.*

I'M A FREAK, YOU'RE A FREAK. YOUR SHUT-IN UNCLE IS NUTS, AND MY SHUT-IN DAD IS A LUNATIC. SO I DON'T KNOW WHAT YOU THINK MAKES US SO DIFFERENT.

I'M TRYING TO SEE THAT AS A COMPLIMENT.

I TOLD LENA IT WAS NO BIG DEAL THAT SHE WAS — WHAT? A WITCH? A CASTER?

YEAH, NO BIG DEAL.

I'M A BIG LIAR.

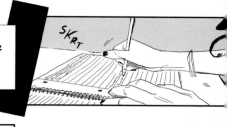

SKRT

BUT EVER SINCE THEN, I ONLY EVER WANT TO BE WITH LENA.

SHE ISN'T MY GIRLFRIEND, I DON'T EVEN KNOW HOW SHE FEELS ABOUT ME. WE DON'T DATE. BUT I WANT TO.

IT DIDN'T TAKE LONG FOR WORD TO GET OUT THAT "OLD MAN RAVENWOOD'S NIECE" WAS HANGING OUT WITH "ETHAN WATE WHOSE MAMMA DIED JUST LAST YEAR."

STOP & SHOP

DING

NO WAY!

HUH?

WHAT?

LARKIN! STOP THAT!

HIS... ARM...

GEEZ. JUST TRYIN' TO LIFT THE MOOD.

SO, CUZ, ANY BIG PLANS FOR YOUR BIRTHDAY?

RIDLEY, THAT'S ENOUGH.

I SPENT JUST AS MUCH TIME WITH YOU AS LENA DID, UNCLE M. HOW DID SHE BECOME YOUR FAVORITE?

YOU HAVE BEEN CLAIMED. IT'S OUT OF MY HANDS.

CLAIMED?

RUMMBLE

PATTA

PATTER

DIZZY...

SQUEEZE

IN A FEW MONTHS, YOU COULD END UP EXACTLY LIKE ME, LENA. DON'T YOU THINK BOYFRIEND HERE DESERVES TO KNOW EVERYTHING? THAT YOU HAVE NO IDEA IF YOU'RE LIGHT OR DARK? THAT YOU HAVE NO CHOICE?

SHUT UP!

I'M SO COLD...   EVERYTHING'S FROZEN...

CHAPTER 3

WE'LL FIGURE SOMETHING OUT.

AFTER LEAVING RAVENWOOD MANOR, ALL I WANT IS TO RETURN TO LENA.

UGH, I CAN'T SLEEP.

THMP

WHAT?

TMP TMP TMP

SNEAK

WHERE IS AMMA GOING IN THE MIDDLE OF THE NIGHT?

CRRK

NONSENSE. I RAISED THAT CHILD. DON'T YOU THINK I'D KNOW IT IF HE HAD ANY KIND OF POWER?

YOU'RE WRONG THIS TIME. I'M WARNING YOU, THERE IS MORE TO THE BOY THAN EITHER OF US REALIZED.

VRRMMM

I HEARD YOU LIKE DONUTS. I COULD HEAR YOUR STOMACH GROWLING ALL THE WAY FROM RAVENWOOD.

I'VE NEVER SEEN HER SO HAPPY... SHE DOESN'T KNOW ABOUT MACON AND AMMA. BUT I HAVE TO TELL HER.

NO NUMBER ON HER HAND TODAY. HER BIRTHDAY... 120 DAYS...

THAT DOESN'T MAKE ANY SENSE. WHY IS HE MEETING AMMA IN THE MIDDLE OF THE NIGHT TO TELL HER WE HAVE THE LOCKET?

WHY DON'T THEY WANT US TO HAVE IT? THERE'S SOMETHING THEY DON'T WANT US TO KNOW.

WE NEED TO FIND OUT WHAT HAPPENS NEXT.

BURNING A HOUSE WITH WOMEN IN IT.

IT CAN'T BE TRUE!

TMP
TMP
THMP

SHFF

FWOOM

WHAT THE—?

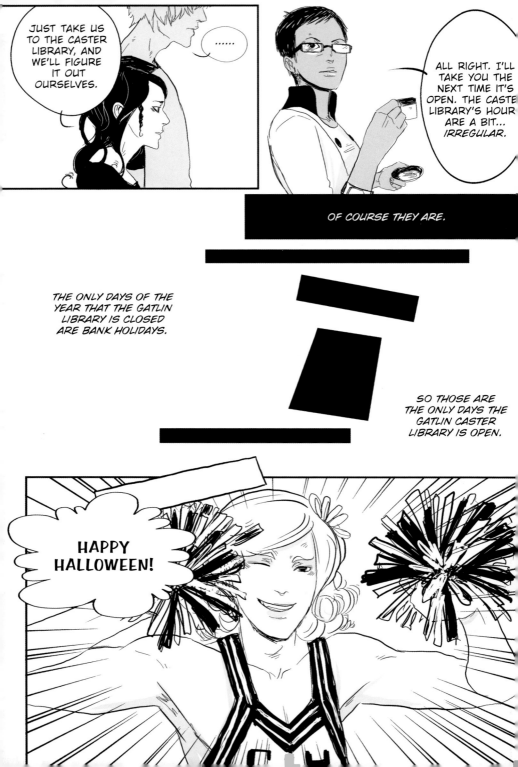

I DON'T CARE.

I CAN HANDLE THIS.

hol

WHATEVER HAPPENS TO YOU, HAPPENS TO ME.

THEY REALLY HATE ME...

They Really Hate You

Yes They Do!

=HAHA

HEY, DO YOU HAVE ANY MAKEUP REMOVER?

THIS ISN'T COMIN' OFF. I THOUGHT YOU SAID THIS COMES OFF WITH WATER.

IT DOES.

THEN WHY ISN'T IT COMIN' OFF?!

LOOKS LIKE THEY'RE HAVING SOME KIND OF PROBLEM.

WHAT THE—?

I HAVE RELATIVES COMING IN FROM ALL OVER, AND UNCLE M WON'T LET ME OUT OF THE HOUSE FOR FIVE MINUTES. NOT TO MENTION THE DANGER.

I NEVER THOUGHT OF IT THAT WAY.

I'D NEVER OPEN MY DOOR TO A STRANGER ON A NIGHT OF SUCH DARK POWER.

A NIGHT OF SUCH DARK POWER...

CHAPTER 4

THE BOY PROTECTS HER. I'VE NEVER SEEN ANYTHING LIKE IT. NO CASTER CAN COME BETWEEN THEM.

BUT SARAFINE'S POWERS ARE GROWING BY THE DAY.

WE CAN'T STOP HER FROM COMING FOR LENA.

SLUMP

striking us

AFTER HALLOWEEN...

YOUR HOUSE WAS FULL OF THESE CREEPY PEOPLE WHO LOOKED LIKE THEY WERE AT A COSTUME PARTY.

HEH.

AND THEN YOU FOUND ME? YOU RODE IN ON YOUR WHITE STALLION AND SAVED ME?

DON'T JOKE. IT WAS REALLY SCARY. AND THERE WAS NO STALLION, IT WAS MORE LIKE A DOG.

...IT FELT LIKE THE CALM AFTER THE STORM. WE SETTLED INTO A ROUTINE, BUT...

...WE KNEW THE CLOCK WAS TICKING.

NO SIGNS OF FLIRTY SIRENS.

NO UNEXPLAINED CATEGORY 3 STORMS.

THEN THE UNTHINKABLE HAPPENED.

FREEZE

I CAN'T MOVE.

EVERYONE FROZE!

ETHAN? ARE YOU ALL RIGHT?!

DID I DO THIS?

CAST A TIME BIND? NO, YOU DIDN'T DO THIS, CHILD.

"Gasp."

THE GREATS FIGURED IT WAS TIME WE HAD OURSELVES A TALK, WOMAN TO WOMAN. NOBODY CAN HEAR US NOW.

EXCEPT ME, I CAN HEAR.

ARE YOU A CASTER?

NO, I'M JUST A SEER.

HUH?

AN UNDERGROUND PASSAGE?!

FWOOF

CAN'T WAIT!

TMP

LET'S GO...

LENA LOOKS LIKE SHE CAN ALREADY FEEL THE MAGIC OF THIS PLACE.

WHAT I WAS FEELING WAS LESS MAGICAL.

ETHAN...

I'M SORRY, CHILD. HE'S GONE.

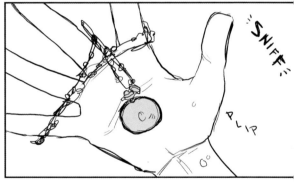

SNIFF

FLIP

?!!

THE BOOK OF MOONS HAS BEEN MISSING FOR OVER A HUNDRED YEARS...

ON MONDAY, LINK AND I PICKED LENA UP AT THE FORK IN THE ROAD. LINK LIKED LENA, BUT THERE'S NO WAY THAT HE'S GOING TO DRIVE RIGH UP TO RAVENWOOD MANOR. IT'S STIL A HAUNTED MANSION TO HIM.

BUT ACCORDING TO LINK, THERE WAS TROUBLE OF ANOTHER KIND BREWING. HIS MOM HAD BEEN WHISPERING ON THE PHONE FOR THE PAST TWENTY-FOUR HOURS. WHEN LINK LISTENED IN, HE DIDN'T CATCH MUCH, BUT IT WAS ENOUGH TO FIGURE OUT HIS MOM'S END GAME.

"WE'LL GET HER OUTTA OUR SCHOOL, ONE WAY OR ANOTHER."

AND HER LITTLE DOG TOO.

SO, WHEN ARE YOU GONNA WRITE ME A SONG?

HAHA

RIGHT AFTER I FINISH THE ONE I'M WRITING FOR BOB DYLAN.

HOLY CRAP.

FREEZE

BLUE

?

NOW THERE'S A TERRIFYING SIGHT.

MY MOM!

DECEMBER MEANS ONLY ONE THING AT JACKSON HIGH: THE WINTER FORMAL.

IT WAS PRETTY OBVIOUS LENA WANTED TO BE ASKED. IT WAS LIKE SHE HAD A LIST OF ALL THE THINGS SHE IMAGINED A REGULAR GIRL WAS SUPPOSED TO DO IN HIGH SCHOOL, AND SHE WAS DETERMINED TO DO THEM.

THIS IS MY YEAR. I CAN FEEL IT. I'M GONNA GET SNOW KING THIS YEAR.

WHAT IS THAT, LIKE AN AFTER-SCHOOL SPECIAL?

YOUR GIRLFRIEND THINKS THAT I'M SPECIAL, DUDE.

IS THAT WHAT I AM?

IS THAT WHAT YOU WANT TO BE?

ARE YOU ASKING ME SOMETHING?

I GUESS I AM.

THEN I GUESS I'M YOUR GIRLFRIEND. ♥

JUST LIKE THAT, I NOT ONLY HAVE A DATE TO THE WINTER FORMAL, I HAVE A GIRLFRIEND.

AND NOT JUST A GIRLFRIEND. FOR THE FIRST TIME IN MY LIFE, I ALMOST USED THE "L" WORD.

WHAT THE HECK ARE THOSE?!

THEY'RE BABY SQUIRRELS.

AND YOU WATCH YOUR LANGUAGE.

WHAT IF THE BOOK OF MOONS IS BURIED SOMEWHERE?

MAYBE WITH THE PERSON WHO UNDERSTOOD ITS POWER BETTER THAN ANYONE.

LENA! I THINK I KNOW WHERE THE BOOK IS!

I THINK IT'S WITH GENEVIEVE.

GENEVIEVE IS DEAD.

I KNOW.

WHAT ARE YOU SAYING, ETHAN?

I THINK YOU KNOW WHAT I'M SAYING.

WHERE DO YOU THINK HER GRAVE IS?

THIS IS IT, ETHAN. I CAN FEEL IT.

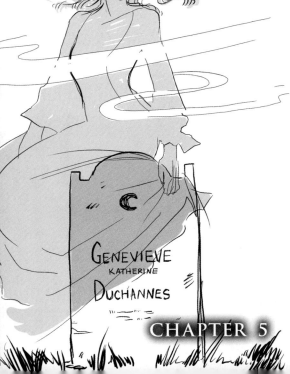

GASP!

ETHAN, CAN YOU SEE HER?!

YEAH.

GENEVIEVE. IT'S HER. MAYBE THIS IS A MISTAKE...

GENEVIEVE
KATHERINE
DUCHANNES

CHAPTER 5

TRY NOT TO LOOK AT HER... SHE KEEPS STARING AT US WITH THOSE VACANT GOLD EYES...

& CREEPY...?

GRP

DIGGING UP A GRAVE UNDER A FULL MOON...! THIS IS SCARY. NOT RAVENWOOD SCARY. OR RIDLEY-TRYING-TO-KILL-ME SCARY... THIS IS LIKE THE THOUGHT OF LOSING LENA.

PARALYZING FEAR.

SKJFF

WHAT WAS I THINKING?!

SCRFF

You were trying to right a wrong.

Take it.

SHE WANTS US TO TAKE THE BOOK.

WE FOUND IT!

AND GENEVIEVE'S GONE.

OUCH!

THUMP

IT BURNS!!

WHAT PART OF "ONLY A CASTER CAN TOUCH THIS BOOK" AREN'T YOU GETTING?

RIGHT. THAT PART.

EVERY TIME I TOUCH IT, MY HANDS BURN. IT'S LIKE WHEN I TOUCH LENA AND FEEL AN ELECTRIC SHOCK.

BUT WORSE.

HUNDREDS OF CASTS IN ENGLISH, LATIN, GAELIC, AND OTHER LANGUAGES...

DOES ANY OF THIS MEAN ANYTHING TO YOU?

NO. IN MY FAMILY, BEFORE YOUR CLAIMING YOU AREN'T REALLY ALLOWED TO KNOW ANYTHING.

IN CASE YOU GO DARK...

...I GUESS

THESE PAGES ARE IN ENGLISH. SOMEONE STARTED TO TRASLATE IT IN THE BACK.

THE CLAYMING, ONCE BOUND, CANNOT BE UNBOUND. THE CHOICE, ONCE CAST, CANNOT BE RECAST. A PERSON OF POWERE FALLES INTO THE GREAT DARKENING OR THE GREAT LIGHT, FOR ALL TYME. IF TYME PASSES AND THE LASTE HOURE OF THE SIXTEENTHE MOONE FLEES UNBOUND, THE ORDER OF THINGS IS UNDONE. THIS MUST NOT BE. THE BOOKE WILLE BINDE THAT WHICHE IS UNBOUND FOR ALL TYME.

SO THERE'S REALLY NO GETTING AROUND THIS CLAIMING THING?

THAT'S WHAT I'VE BEEN TELLING YOU.

I'M NOT WORRIED.

ME NEITHER.

HA-HA-HA!

AT LEAST THE WINTER FORMAL MIGHT DISTRACT US A LITTLE...

IT'S BEAUTIFUL!

BUT I GUESS TO LENA, THAT'S SOMETHING BEAUTIFUL.

HONESTLY, IT ISN'T BEAUTIFUL.

LET'S GET THIS PARTY STARTED!

NO WAY.

HEY, CUZ!

LINK!

GRAB

WHAT ARE YOU DOING WITH RIDLEY?!

DUDE, CAN YOU BELIEVE IT? SHE'S THE HOTTEST CHICK IN GATLIN!

I FELT SORRY FOR WHOEVER THEY WOULD BLAME FOR THIS MESS...

BUT OF COURSE—

AFTERWARD, I HEARD...

...MRS. LINCOLN FOUND SOMEONE TO BLAME.

HOW COULD MRS. LINCOLN BLAME LENA?!

WHY DOES SHE HAVE IT IN FOR HER?!

THAT RAVENWOOD GIRL!

SHE PULLED THE FIRE ALARM AND DESTROYED EVERYTHING!

IT'S...INSANE.

54 DAYS LEFT.

"AMONGST PERSONNES OF POWERE, THERE BEING TWINNE FORCES FROM PHYCHE SPRING LL MAGICK, THE ARKNESSE AND THE LIGHT."

YOU THINK WE CAN SKIP TO THE GOOD PART? LIKE, LOOPHOLES FOR YOUR CLAIMING DAY?

IT GETS REALLY COMPLICATED. I'M NOT SURE I UNDERSTAND...

LENA...

SHE SHUT ME OUT. I CAN'T HEAR HER THOUGHTS OR TALK TO HER...

HEY, MAN.

I GOT A FAVOR TO ASK YOU.

SURE.

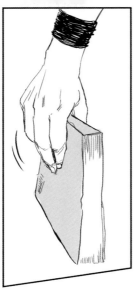

"WHAT IS THE OPPOSITE OF TWO? A LONELY ME, A LONELY YOU."

WEIRD. THAT'S EXACTLY HOW I FEEL.

WHEN I WALKED IN THIS MORNING, THESE BOOKS WERE IN A PILE ON THE FLOOR. I DON'T KNOW HOW THEY GOT THERE.

I SAT DOWN TO LOOK THROUGH THEM, AND EVERY SINGLE BOOK HAD SOME KIND OF MESSAGE FOR ME.

YOU TRY. OPEN ONE.

......

shakespeare

SHAKESPEARE, JULIUS CAESAR.

"MEN AT SOME TIMES ARE MASTERS OF THEIR FATES: THE FAULT, DEAR BRUTUS, IS NOT IN OUR STARS, BUT IN OURSELVES, THAT WE ARE UNDERLINGS."

WHAT DOES THAT HAVE TO DO WITH ME?

THE THING ABOUT FATE IS, ARE YOU THE MASTER OF YOUR FATE, OR ARE THE STARS?

MAYBE IT'S TIME TO CONFRONT MY FATE, AND LENA'S FATE. WHETHER IT'S UP TO US OR THE STARS, I CAN'T JUST SIT AROUND AND WAIT TO FIND OUT.

DECEMBER 23

THERE WAS
SOMETHING IN
THE AIR.

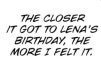

THE CLOSER
IT GOT TO LENA'S
BIRTHDAY, THE
MORE I FELT IT.

DECEMBER 25

JANUARY 1

JANUARY 15

AT NIGHT WE
STAYED UP LATE
TALKING.

JANUARY 30

EVERY NIGHT SEEMED CLOSER TO THE
NIGHT THAT COULD BE OUR LAST.

FEBRUARY 4

WHAT IS HE HIDING...?

NO MATTER HOW HARD WE TRIED, WE COULDN'T FIND ANYTHING IN THE BOOK OF MOONS.

CLAK

NOW WHAT?

SO, I HEAR IT'S LENA'S BIRTHDAY TOMORROW.

RIDLEY TOLD ME.

YOU TWO ARE STILL HANGING OUT?

YEAH, MAN. CAN YOU KEEP A SECRET?

HAVEN'T I ALWAYS?

TATTOO?!

I GOT IT OVER CHRISTMAS BREAK. PRETTY COOL, HUH? RIDLEY DREW IT HERSELF.

SHE'S A KILLER ARTIST!

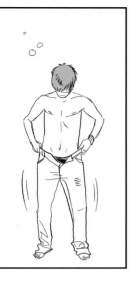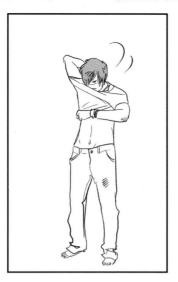

EVEN THOUGH WE NEVER FOUND ANYTHING, I BETTER BRING THE BOOK.

SHFF

WHAT?

THE BOOK OF MOONS...

...OUR BOOK...

...IS GONE.

TODAY OF ALL DAYS!!

CHAPTER 6

Sixteen moons, sixteen years
Sixteen of your deepest fears
Sixteen times you dreamed my tears
Falling, falling through the years...

Sixteen moons, sixteen years
Sound of thunder in your ears
Sixteen miles before she nears
Sixteen seeks what sixteen fears...

Sixteen moons, sixteen years
Sixteen times you dreamed my fears,
Sixteen will try to Bind the spheres,
Sixteen screams but just one hears...

Sixteen moons, sixteen years
The Claiming moon, the hour nears,
In these pages Darkness clears,
Powers Bind what fire sears...

Sixteenth Moon, Sixteenth Year
Now has come the day you fear,
Claim or be Claimed,
Shed blood, shed tear,
Moon or Sun—destroy, revere...

YOU SHOULD ALREADY KNOW THE ANSWER.

CLASP

IT REALLY FEELS LIKE ELECTRICITY.

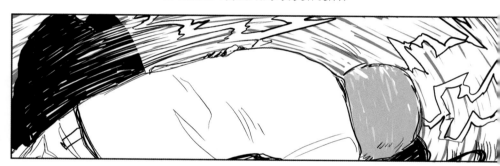

WHEN WE KISS LIKE THIS, IT ALMOST HURTS.

Haah

CRINGE

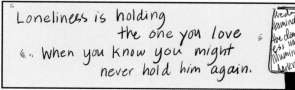

Loneliness is holding the one you love ... when you know you might never hold him again.

WE STAYED IN HER ROOM
AS LONG AS WE COULD.
LENA DIDN'T WANT TO GO
DOWNSTAIRS.

BUT...

...MACON KEPT
CALLING UP
TO HER. WE
COULDN'T AVOID
IT FOREVER.

I GUESS WE
HAVE TO GO DOWN
THERE AND SEE
MY FAMILY.

WHAT...?

ETHAN, ARE YOU OKAY?

MY DAD IS...

ETHAN, DID YOU HEAR ME?

B...BUT... I CAN'T LEAVE LENA ALONE...

COME ON, MAN!

ETHAN!

.......! LARKIN!

?

I NEED YOU TO TAKE LENA BACK TO THE HOUSE!

...? SURE, MAN. I'LL TAKE HER BACK NOW.

I ALREADY LOST MY MOM... I KNOW MY DAD IS CRAZY, BUT I LOVE HIM. I CAN'T LOSE HIM TOO...!

DIDN'T YOU HEAR WHAT YOUR FRIEND SAID? I'M A WITCH. A BAD ONE.

THAT LOOK ON HIS FACE. THIS IS PROBABLY THE FIRST TIME LINK IS REALLY SEEING HER.

BUT YOU AREN'T ALL BAD. I KNOW THAT. WE'VE SHARED THINGS.

GASP

THAT WAS THE PLAN, HOT ROD. I NEEDED AN IN.

SO I COULD STAY CLOSE TO LENA.

I DON'T BELIEVE YOU...

LINK...WHATEVER SPELL RIDLEY CAST, HIS FEELINGS FOR HER ARE BIGGER THAN THAT.

WHAT ABOUT EVERYTHING YOU TOLD ME ABOUT YOU AND LENA GROWIN' UP TOGETHER?

WHY WOULD YOU WANT TO HURT HER?

LIKE I SAID, THIS IS MY JOB. GET ETHAN AWAY FROM LENA. THIS OLD GUY WAS JUST AN EASY TARGET.

HIS MIND IS WEAK.

"GET ETHAN AWAY FROM LENA."

THAT'S WHAT THIS IS ABOUT?

RID, DON'T DO IT!

DAD!

WHAT IS HE SAYING?? I CAN'T HEAR.

......

3HFF

SOMETHING'S WRONG...

NO, WAIT. THAT'S NOT MRS. LINCOLN.

CHAPTER 7

KNOW WHAT?!

YOUR UNCLE DIDN'T TELL YOU.

YOU AND ETHAN CAN NEVER BE TOGETHER, NOT PHYSICALLY.

CASTERS AND LILUM CANNOT BE WITH MORTALS.

AT LEAST NOT WITHOUT KILLING THEM.

CASTERS CANNOT BE WITH MORTALS WITHOUT KILLING THEM.

YOU CAN NEVER MARRY, NEVER HAVE CHILDREN. YOU CAN NEVER HAVE A FUTURE.

NO... THAT'S WHY THERE'S THAT ELECTRICITY WHENEVER WE TOUCH?!

LENA...

UNCLE MACON...

I NEVER REALIZED HOW STRONG MACON IS...THAT TREE SNAPPED IN HALF!

?!

SHFF

CHOMP

!!

LINK!
COME ON!

IT'S ALMOST MIDNIGHT.

AUNT
DEL!

REECE!
GRAMMA!

HELLO?
WHERE IS
EVERYBODY?

TMP

ETHAN?!

LENA DISAPPEARED,
AND WHEN MACON DIDN'T
COME BACK, WE BEGAN
TO WORRY! HAVE YOU
SEEN THEM?

...I CAN'T SEE ANYONE IN THIS SMOKE!

NOT HUNTING, LARKIN, SARAFINE... LENA...!

ETHAN! I'M UP HERE.

ON TOP OF THE CRYPT. BUT I THINK I'M STUCK.

COUGH

WHAT?

INSIDE THE CRYPT.

THE BOOK OF MOONS?!

HOLD ON, L. I'M COMING.

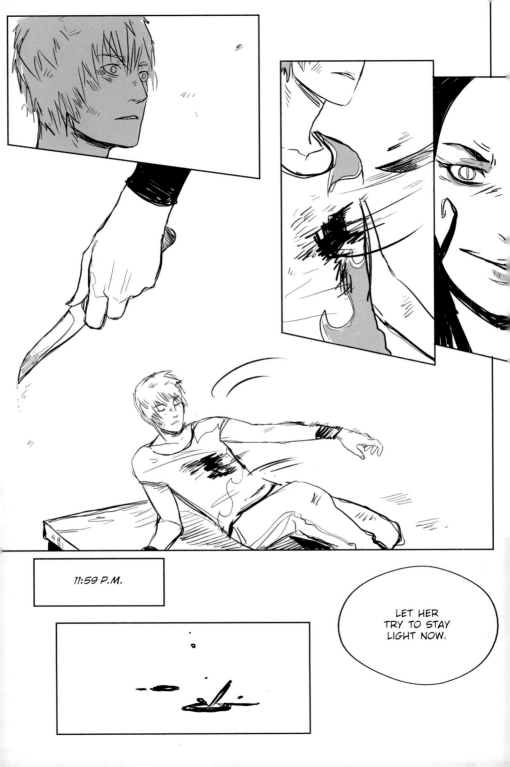

11:59 P.M.

LET HER
TRY TO STAY
LIGHT NOW.

ETHAN!
NO!

NO

NO

NO

THIS CAN'T BE HAPPENING!

EVERYTHING IS...
FROZEN.

......
......

ETHAN,
I LOVE YOU.
DON'T
LEAVE ME!!

THE
WORDS...

THE WORDS
FROM THE
VISIONS!

CHAPTER 8

ETHAN!

IF UNCLE MACON IS HERE, THEN ETHAN...!

HE'S...
HE'S SO
COLD TOO.

WHAT HAVE I DONE?

I WON'T SAY GOOD-BYE! I WON'T SAY IT!

I LOST THEM BOTH!

I'M NOT GOING ANYWHERE.

AND NEITHER ARE YOU.

LENA TOLD ME WHAT HAD HAPPENED WHILE I WAS PASSED OUT...

MACON WAS THE ONLY CASUALTY. APPARENTLY, HUNTING OVERPOWERED HIM AFTER I LOST CONSCIOUSNESS.

MACON ALWAYS SAID HE WOULD DO ANYTHING FOR LENA. HE WAS A MAN OF HIS WORD.

AND SARAFINE...

I'M FUZZY ON THE
DETAILS, BUT LENA SOMEHOW
MANAGED TO BLOCK OUT THE
MOON AND SAVE HERSELF
FROM BEING CLAIMED.

WITHOUT THE CLAIMING,
IT LOOKS LIKE SARAFINE,
HUNTING, AND LARKIN FLED,
AT LEAST FOR NOW.

AND THEN THERE'S ME.
I GUESS I FELL WHILE
CLIMBING THAT CRYPT AND
KNOCKED MYSELF OUT.

LIKE AN IDIOT.

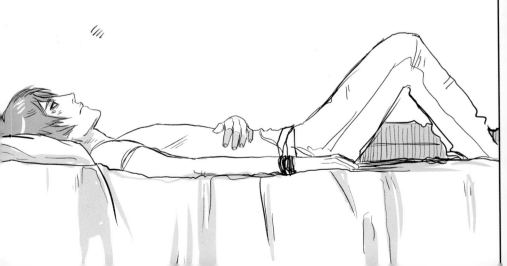

ONE EYE IS GREEN.

AND THE OTHER IS...GOLD.

NEVER.

CRNCH

DON'T LET GO.

AUNT DEL OFFERED TO DRIVE ME HOME, BUT I WANTED TO WALK.

I NEED TO CLEAR MY HEAD...

I STILL CAN'T BELIEVE WE LOST MACON.

THE RIGHT THING
AND THE EASY THING
ARE NEVER THE SAME.
NO ONE KNEW THAT
BETTER THAN MACON.

A NEW SONG?

?

......
......

Seventeen moons, seventeen years.
Eyes where Dark or Light appears.
Gold for yes and Green for no.
Seventeen the last to know.

THE END

BEAUTIFUL CREATURES:

KAMI GARCIA & MARGARET STOHL
CASSANDRA JEAN

Adaptation and Illustration:
Cassandra Jean

Lettering: Abigail Blackman

PENGUIN BOOKS

Published by the Penguin Group
Penguin Books Ltd, 80 Strand, London WC2R 0RL, England
Penguin Group (USA) Inc., 375 Hudson Street, New York,
New York 10014, USA
Penguin Group (Canada), 90 Eglinton Avenue East,
Suite 700, Toronto, Ontario, Canada M4P 2Y3
(a division of Pearson Penguin Canada Inc.)
Penguin Ireland, 25 St Stephen's Green, Dublin 2, Ireland (a
division of Penguin Books Ltd)
Penguin Group (Australia), 707 Collins Street, Melbourne,
Victoria 3008, Australia
(a division of Pearson Australia Group Pty Ltd)
Penguin Books India Pvt Ltd, 11 Community Centre,
Panchsheel Park, New Delhi – 110 017, India
Penguin Group (NZ), 67 Apollo Drive, Rosedale,
Auckland 0632, New Zealand
(a division of Pearson New Zealand Ltd)
Penguin Books (South Africa) (Pty) Ltd, Block D, Rosebank
Office Park, 181 Jan Smuts Avenue,
Parktown North, Gauteng 2193, South Africa

Penguin Books Ltd, Registered Offices: 80 Strand,
London WC2R 0RL, England

penguin.com

Adapted from the novel *Beautiful Creatures*,
published in Great Britain in Razorbill,
an imprint of Penguin Books 2010
Published in the USA by Yen Press,
an imprint of Hachette Book Group, Inc. 2013
Published simultaneously in Great Britain
by Penguin Books 2013
002

Text copyright © Kami Garcia and Margaret Stohl, 2009
Illustrations copyright © Hachette Book Group,
Inc., 2013
Adaptation and illustration by Cassandra Jean
Lettering by Abigail Blackman
All rights reserved

The moral right of the author and illustrator
has been asserted

Printed in Italy by Graphicom

British Library Cataloguing in Publication Data
A CIP catalogue record for this book is available
from the British Library

ISBN: 978–0–141–34851–3

KAMI GARCIA and **MARGARET STOHL** came up with the concept for *Beautiful Creatures*, their debut novel, over lunch. Margaret had always been captivated by fantasies and wanted to write a supernatural novel, while Kami loved stories set in the South and wanted to write a book that drew upon her deep Southern roots. With nothing to write on, they scribbled their ideas for a story that combined their shared passions on a paper napkin. By the time they left, *Beautiful Creatures* was born. Kami and Margaret both live in Los Angeles, California, with their families. They now write on computers instead of napkins, and invite you to visit them online at www.kamigarciamargaretstohl.com.

CASSANDRA JEAN is a freelance illustrator and comic artist who spends her days toiling with a pen in her hand, and her faithful dog sleeping at her feet. The radio is always on and Gatorade is a constant source of power!